P9-DOA-575

For all those lost at sea
For Kate Agnew and Mairi Kidd with love
For my dear friend Jane Ray for creating these beautiful pictures,
the like of which I never saw when I was a child – SB

For Sita Brahmachari, and all our friends at The Islington Centre
for Refugees and Migrants, in celebration of the power
of Art and Writing – JR

In researching the illustrations for this book, I looked at the familiar ancient Celtic knot design (pp42-43), wanting to include it somewhere in the imagery, as being deeply symbolic of the Orcadian culture that Isla's mother was born into. I was delighted to discover that the same design features in the traditional beadwork of the Yoruba people of Nigeria, where Isla's grandparents on her father's side originate from. Such connection across continents and cultures seemed to sum up completely the message of Sita's beautiful story.
Jane Ray

Acknowledgements
Lines from *A New Child* copyright © George Mackay Brown 1996
are reproduced by permission of Hodder and Stoughton Limited

First published in Great Britain in 2018 and in the USA in 2019 by
Otter-Barry Books, Little Orchard, Burley Gate, Herefordshire, HR1 3QS
www.otterbarrybooks.com

A catalogue record for this book is available from the British Library.

ISBN 978-1-91095-997-8

Printed in China
1 3 5 7 9 8 6 4 2

Corey's Rock

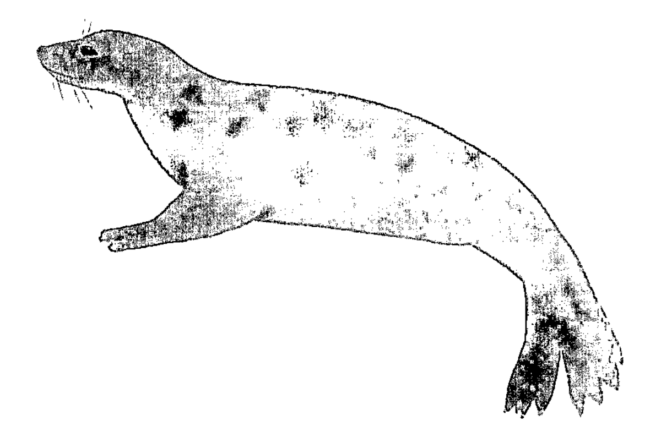

Written by Sita Brahmachari

Illustrated by Jane Ray

We stand on the grey rock
of our new home.
The four of us.
At sunset.
Four is an even number,
Mum, Dad, me and Sultan.
But everything feels odd.
Stroking Sultan's head
and watching the surface
where nothing breaks
but waves.

"Time to say goodbye," Mum says.

She hands me petals, and more to Dad.

We raise our hands to scatter them across the sea.

The rose that's supposed to mean we say goodbye

to Corey.

My brother.

We watch him float away.

A petal for every birthday.

One by one by one by one by one.

Five red petals blur the fire horizon.

"We'll call this Corey's rock," Dad says.

I follow the red dots far out to the world's end,
calling for Corey.
My voice,
the wind's voice,
the sea's sway,
all melt away and the petals grow heavy and sink
into the inky depths.

"Corey," I call.
I hit my head against the bedpost.
Through bleary eyes I search for the reason I am here,
where nothing is where it should be,
not even the door.
The windows have shrunk into
painted brick walls.
I lift my head from my pillow.

And now I remember the
half-unpacked trunk in the corner,
below the window with the curtain of yellow daffodils
that only make me feel sadder.
Corey loved daffodils.

I creak down the rickety stairs
where Mum and Dad sit close in the fire's glow,
steam rising from their cups,
Sultan warming their feet.
Mum reading, Dad sleeping.
The TV is turned to silent.
These are the things we did in our old flat with Corey,
but now they seem strange,
as if we're pretending he never was.

My eyes are caught by a rolling wave.
Am I still dreaming?
On the screen
seals wash in, swash in, from the sea.
Fishermen rush to the shore,
not with nets but with blankets.
Dad stirs and watches the passing pictures,
searching for the remote. He mutters,
"Shipwreck...here I am digging up the ancient boats
and now new ones washing in..."

The seals wash up one by one by one by one.
An old man reaches down and pulls back a skin
and underneath,
my breath flies out of me,
there is a boy's face.
"Corey!" I say his name out loud.

Dad jumps up and hits his head on the roof.
He doesn't fit in our new house.
Now I see that the seals have turned into people,
washed up on the shore.
The fishermen are saving them,
wrapping them in blankets.
"Turn it off, Mosi. I'd like to hide away
and bury my head in poetry."
Now we all sit close on the sofa,
me, Mum and Dad, wrapped in a soft grey blanket,
with Sultan at our feet.
I think maybe Corey will find his way to us,
back across the sea,
through the silence,
and climb up close
so that we can be five again.
Even feels odd.
The screen goes blank.

"Time to sleep now!" Dad says.

He wraps me in the blanket and lifts me high.

"You look as snugly as a seal cub," Mum says.

She smiles, but I don't believe her. Inside she is crying.

She is always crying.

"I saw the Selkies wash in from the sea.... That boy looked like Corey, Dad. Is that why Mum's so sad?"

"I expect so." Dad has to duck to carry me up the stairs.

He looks like a giant in this house.

"I didn't know there were African Selkies..." I sigh as I lay my head down.

Dad strokes my hair like he used to stroke Corey's,
to get him to sleep.
I was the eldest when Corey was alive.
Am I too old for a bedtime story?
If I am then I don't care.
When I listen close I can hear the call of the sea,
see the five red petals floating to me
and the boy-seal with Corey's face
calling....
I close my eyes.
"Tell me the story of the Selkies again," I whisper,
and I am taken away to the sway of Dad's voice.

I am outside the croft,
peering in through the window.
Mum, Dad and Sultan sit by the fire.
'How do you look so cosy?'
I want to scream.
The wind begins to stir,
catching my anger in its roar.
I run along the cliff,
down the winding path,
along the beach to Corey's rock.
The wind smears hair over my face like a veil.
I pull it aside to make a parting.
And there he is, raising his head above the water,
peering out at me,
his huge dark eyes
lit in the moon's glow,
gliding towards me,
his silver back arched and glinting.
I kneel at the water's edge
and stir the salt-sea.
He should have reached me by now.

"Corey!" I call to him over and over.
The wind drops,
the sea grows flat.
No reflections off the water,
no silver backs.
No Selkie skin.
No Corey.

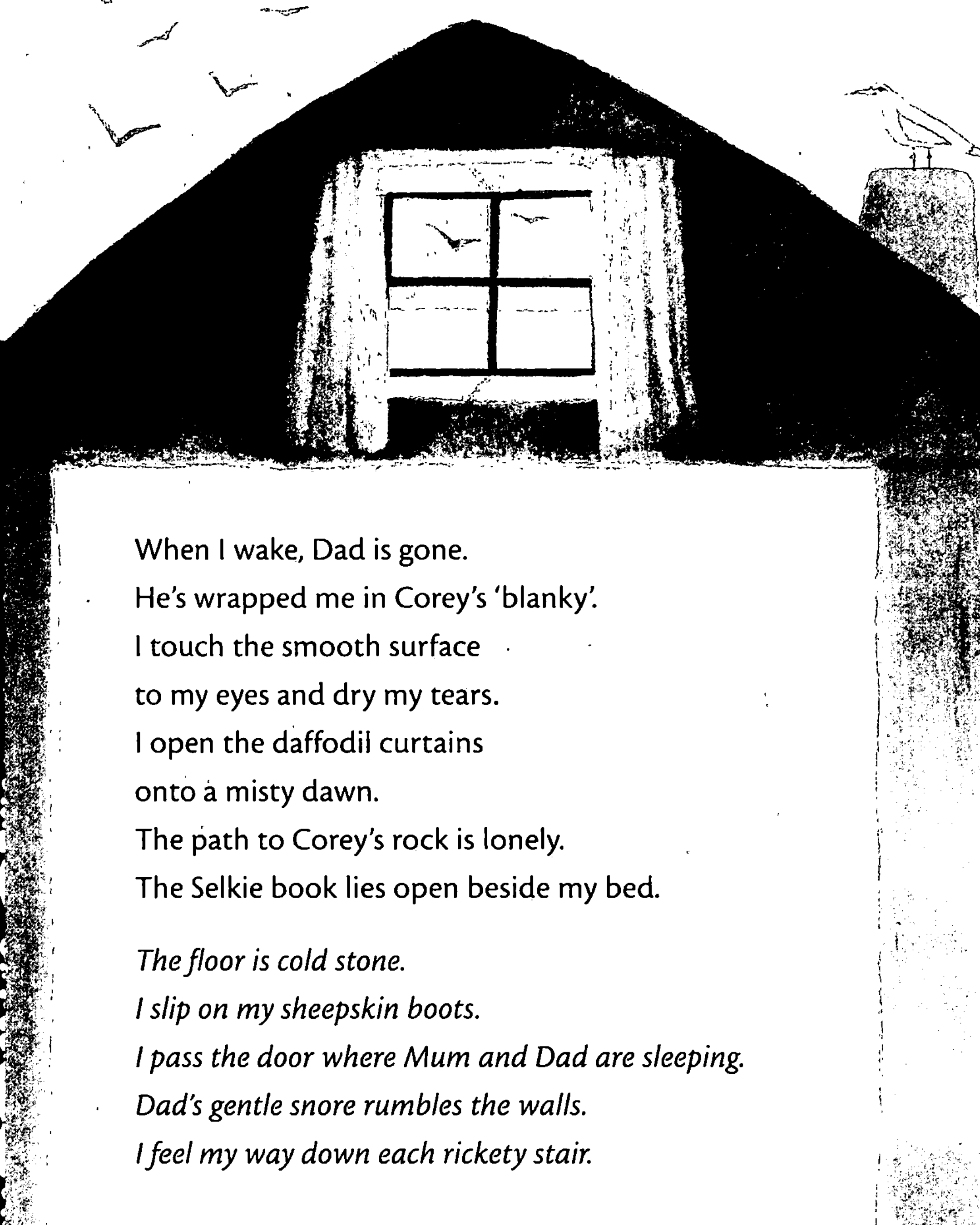

When I wake, Dad is gone.
He's wrapped me in Corey's 'blanky'.
I touch the smooth surface
to my eyes and dry my tears.
I open the daffodil curtains
onto a misty dawn.
The path to Corey's rock is lonely.
The Selkie book lies open beside my bed.

The floor is cold stone.
I slip on my sheepskin boots.
I pass the door where Mum and Dad are sleeping.
Dad's gentle snore rumbles the walls.
I feel my way down each rickety stair.

Sultan whines and waits on the bottom step.
The wood-burner glows
and by the stove my rocking chair is
empty,
but tipping back and forth.
The chair where me and Corey used to curl up rocks
all on its own while the house sleeps.

I open the door.

The sea mist swirls in.

Sultan stands at my heel as I squint down the path.

I take a step

and then another.

Sultan trails my feet,

my feet that are pulling me to Corey's rock.

Faster and faster they draw me along

as if something... someone... needs me.

Over the bank
the full force of the sea blasts,
lifts me like a kite,
propelling me towards Corey's rock,
flying me forward.
The sea is all spray and breaking waves today.
No flatness.
I climb on the rock.
My heart sinks.
Still no Corey waiting for me.
But...

the rock is covered by the strangest skin,
like smooth grey leather.
The underside is velvet,
like the inside of a pea-pod.
I lift it up.
It's as heavy as Corey.
I take it in my arms
and carry it home,
this skin that the sea has shed in place of
red petals
and my brother.

I am wrapped in the day I first held baby Corey.
His birthday,
before we knew
that he wouldn't live for long.
Mum's words at his funeral echo in my head.
"Five years were so much more than we could have
wished for."

I wish for more.
Five red petals is not enough.
I wish that I could hold baby Corey,
that everything could start all over again.

On Corey's rock
a new wave breaks.
One by one by one by one by one the waves roll in,
returning the petals,
and a message.

'Wrap yourself in Selkie skin
Listen to the call within'

I lift the skin and place it on my shoulders.
Then I stand and listen as the waves sing the song of the sea.

'Wrap yourself in Selkie skin
Listen to the call within'

For the longest time nothing breaks the rhyme of the whispering wave.

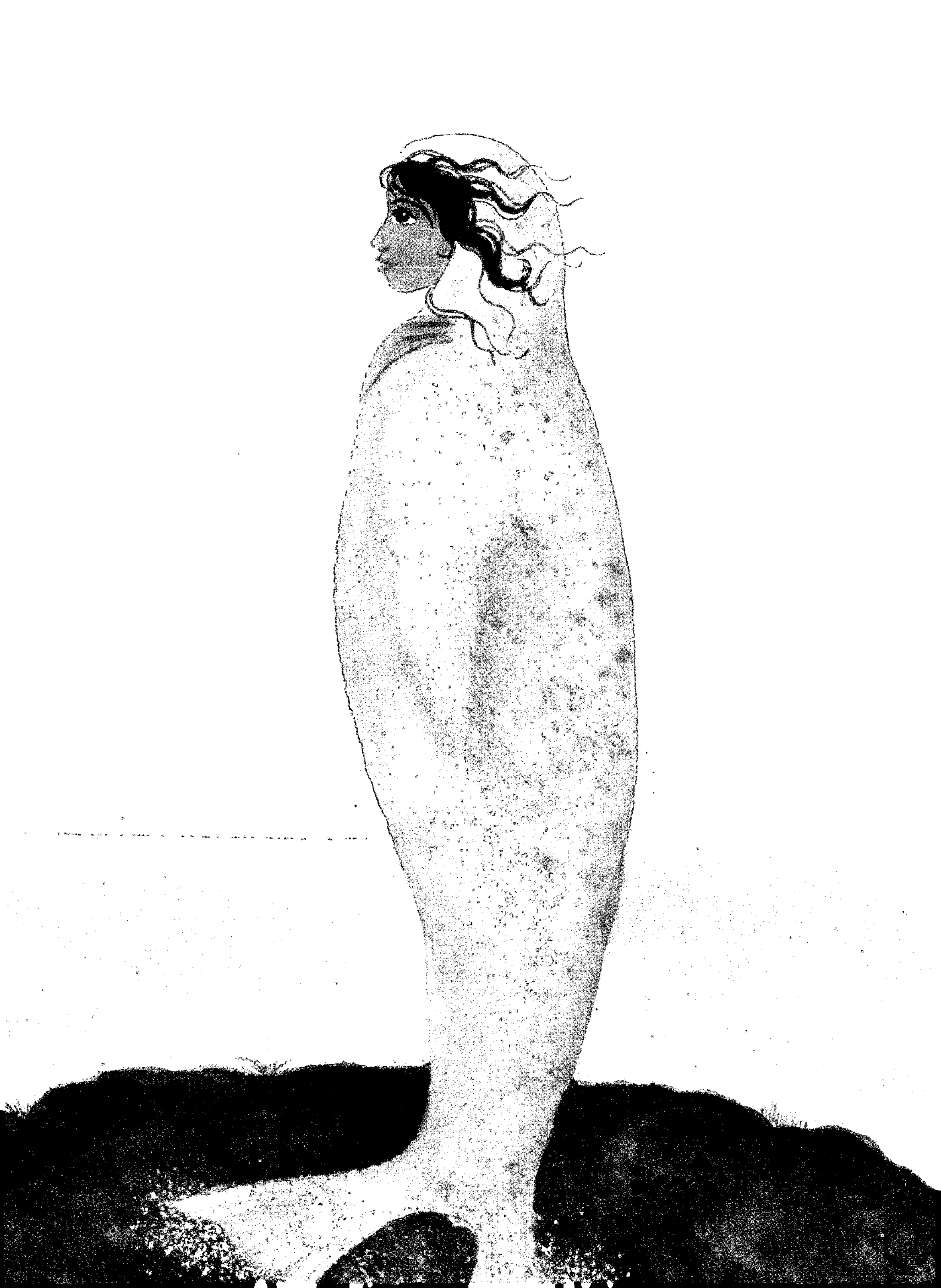

There he is,
bobbing out at sea,
his silken back
surfacing
then disappearing.
I jump down from the rock
and follow him,
running alongside.
There he is,
and there again.
His head peaks the water,
calling,
"Corey, Corey."
Racing the wind.
Racing the waves.

Now here he is, stepping ashore,
coming back to us
to make us all uneven again.
I run to the water,
jump into the waves of ice
and freeze awake.

The door is not where it should be.
The windows are too small.
The trunk is in the corner.
I lift my head from my pillow,
place my feet on the cold stone floor,
open the lid of the trunk
to find
no Selkie skin.

"Our first proper windy walk." Dad spurs me on.
"Who else gets to walk to school along a beach?"
"And over Corey's rock," I say.
"And over Corey's rock," Dad echoes.
We take the sandy path,
the path I walked last night,
carrying the Selkie skin.
The beach is wide and long that curves around
to Corey's rock.
Beyond
leads to my new school.

This was the promise.

"Every day you can walk to school along a beach."

Dad strides on, face to the wind,
my warrior windbreak.
I meander between the scattered rocks.
I miss my street of trees,
the bowing branches outside our old bedroom.
I miss my friend Li-Mei.
I miss...

One by one by one by one by one,
collecting starfish
washed in on the tide,
five at a time.
I return them to the sea.

"Come on, Isla! You'll be late on your first day!"
Dad calls from Corey's rock.
But he's not moving either.
Staring out to sea.
"I can't leave them here! They'll die," I call to him.
One by one by one by one by one.
I return them to the sea.
"You can't save them all!" Dad shouts.
"But they'll die stranded here."

I scramble up the side of the rock
and stand next to him.
"When will Mum come with us back to Corey's rock?"
"When she's ready.... When she's ready."
I don't want to go to a new school.
I don't want to live in a new house.
I don't want a new life without Corey.
I don't care how sick he was.
There it is again, the sea's whisper.

'Wrap yourself in Selkie skin
Listen to the call within'

Dad taps his back and bends down for me to climb on.
He always knows when I need to be carried.

The school is grey-brown stone.
Its name is 'Hope'.
"You'll be just fine here," says Dad.

We find our way to a classroom
and hover outside the door.
A neat-looking teacher with glasses is talking to a class.
She spots us hesitating, waves, opens the door
and steps out.
So this is Miss Lachlan.

As Dad and Miss Lachlan talk I peer inside.
Everyone is staring back.
“Make yourself comfortable.
You’re to sit next to Magnus.”
She points to the only empty chair.
“He’ll be your buddy and show you around.”
I walk the row of staring eyes.
I don’t want to be the new girl.
I want to be back in Edinburgh
with Li-Mei.

I sit next to Magnus.

He has sandy hair, the colour of the beach.

His eyes are grey as Corey's rock.

Dad is hovering in the doorway.

I wish he would go away.

"Just one more thing," he says.

"Could we have a private word?"

Now everyone wants to listen.
I wish he wouldn't tell her anything.
I wish no one here knew that Corey ever existed.

"Now it seems there are two Islas in our class,"
Miss Lachlan announces.
The other Isla waves to me.

"Tell me, how do I pronounce your surname?"
"Abiona," I say slowly so I don't have to repeat it again.
"Abi-ona," Miss Lachlan repeats. "Just to be speedy, do you mind if I call *you* Isla A, and you'll be Isla M?"
I shrug and Isla M smiles at me.
"Now, Isla A. We've been studying the Hindu belief in Reincarnation. We were lucky enough to have a visiting speaker pop in from the archaeological site where your father's working," Miss Lachlan explains. "Now, what was her name...?"
Magnus grins at me.
A bit of his front tooth has chipped off.
Miss Lachlan hands me a Reincarnation worksheet.
"Ah, yes. Mrs Chandran is her name... from India. Have you looked at this belief before?"

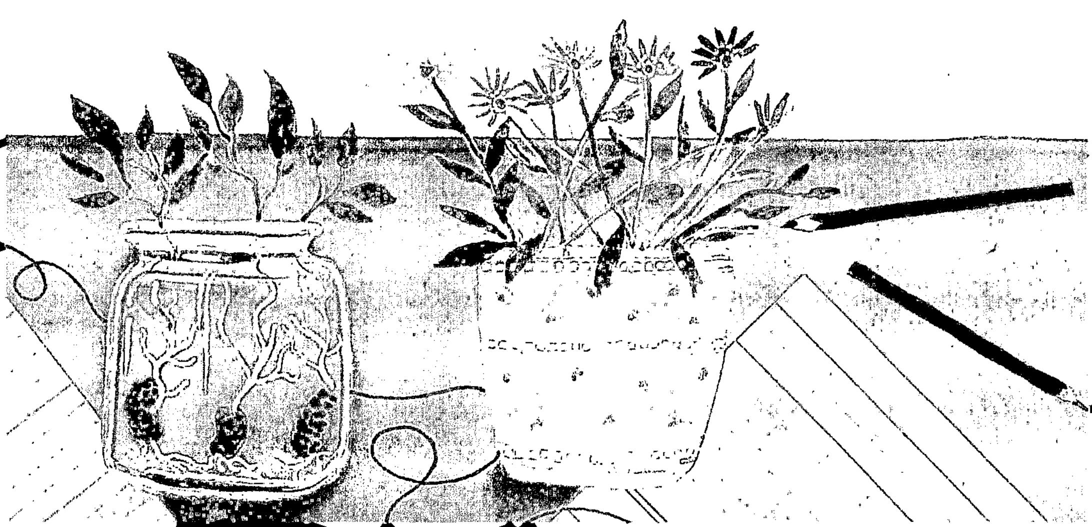

"My friend Li-Mei believes in that," I tell her.
"Well, then. You have a think about what you know and you can tell us all about it next lesson! Mrs Chandran thinks she can feel the past under her feet here. She'll be coming back next week, so you'll meet her then."
Miss Lachlan leans in close to me and whispers.
"By the way, Isla A, saving starfish, wild dreams or no, this is the first and last time you're to be late, OK?"
Magnus slides over a sketchbook to me. He's drawn a picture of Dad standing outside the door. From the strands of his hair he's grown branches.
"Why did you draw him like that?" I ask.
"Because he looks like a great tree...."
"That's true! You're good at art," I tell him.
"Have it!" Magnus says, ripping out the page and writing,

To Isla A, From Magnus P.

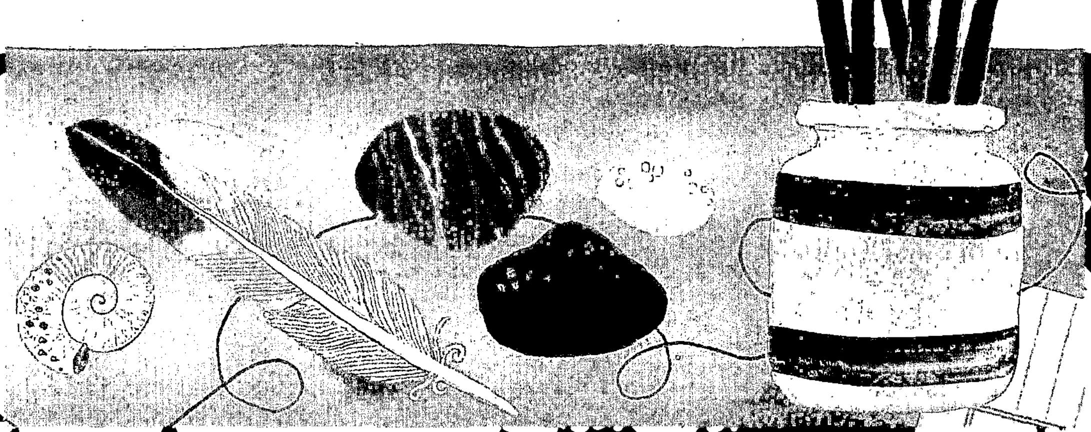

On the way into the playground Magnus P sticks close by me and says,
"My mam says she was at school with your mam and after all you've been through I'm to treat you like family."
We're encircled by girls.
Now the questions start.
"Where are you from?"
"Edinburgh."
"No! But where are you really from?"
"Edinburgh."

"Where's your dad from?"

"Edinburgh."

"Not from Africa?"

"My grandparents were from Africa."

"Have you ever been?"

"Not yet, but my dad says we're going there soon."

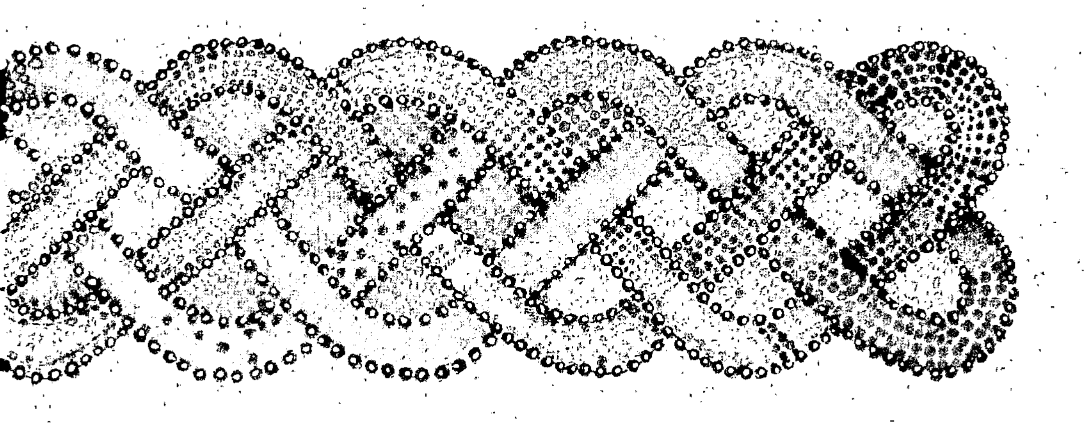

"Stop asking her all these questions." Magnus stands in front of me like my shield.

I don't mind the questions, though. They just want to know me.

"How did you crack your tooth?" I ask Magnus.

"Climbing rocks, how else?"

Outside the school gates Dad is waiting.

"Why can't Mum collect me?"

"She will, when she's in the swing of things."

It's a fair walk from school to the beach.

I don't speak.

"Need a lift?" Dad asks, bending down for me to climb on his back.

I turn to see if anyone is watching.

Magnus stands by the school gates.

"No thanks!" I say, pushing Dad to keep on walking.

"Who's that?"

"Just a boy in my class," I shrug.

The starfish still scatter the beach.

Dad picks up a few, then climbs up onto Corey's rock.

"I think we're going to love it here. Working outside and walking to school."

Dad takes my hand in his.

"If you were to scrape away skin, what would you find? How deep does the colour go?" I ask Dad.

"How deep is the sea?" he answers.

I see red petals floating down and down to the bottom of the ocean and never finding an end.

We stand on the rock, Dad and I,
watching the waves wash in and out
and... wondering.
A sleek head rises from the water and peers at us.
"See that?" I whisper.
Dad holds his hands up to my lips
as the seal lifts its head and peers at us.
For exactly
one, two, three, four, five seconds.
Then it's gone.
"How deep is the sea?" I ask.
Dad's tears drip onto our holding hands.
"As deep as tears," Dad says.
"Come on! Let's go for tea!"
Dad taps his back for me to climb on.
But right now it looks like he's the one who needs
the carrying.
I shake my head and walk beside him.

"Find any treasure?" Mum calls up when she gets in.
"I did! Put my hands in the earth, gave my heart to the wind and my soul to the sky and found a little peace," Dad calls back.
He picks up Mum's poetry book and sings aloud,

'The stories, legends, poems
Will be woven to make you sail,
You may hear the beautiful tale of Magnus
Who took salt on his lip.
Your good angel
Will be with you on that shore.'

Then he reads the title, *A New Child,* by
George Mackay Brown.

I wonder if Dad is teasing me.
But, thinking about it, how would he know
Magnus's name?

"Why did Magnus take salt to his lip? What does that mean?" I ask.

"Haven't a clue! Ask Mum when she comes up. She'll want to find out all about your first day."

"I'm not going to school again."

"And why would that be, my angel?"

"I just want to go home."

"Know what I heard today?" Dad doesn't wait for an answer. He picks up his notebook and begins to read.

'In 1720 a baby boy was found on the shore on Westray after a shipwreck. His name was Archie Angel named after the ship Arch Angel. He lived in Westray for the rest of his life and had many children. Although Angel has died out as a surname it is still used as a middle name.'

"*Our* middle name." Dad looks triumphant as if Angel for a middle name can make me feel at home.
Mum's downstairs, clanking pots.
I wish she would come and say good night to me.
"You think this island will make us happy again?" I ask.
My eyes are teary.
"I hope so, angel."
I wait for the clanking pots to be over. I wait for Mum to hold me close like she used to every night before Corey died.

I run down the stairs,
along the coastal path to the sea.
I scour the horizon, but no seal rises from
the waves.
I kneel at the water's edge and taste.
Salt is on my lip.
Dad's voice fading.
"You may hear the beautiful tale of Magnus
who took salt on his lip. Your good angel."
"There's an angel called Magnus in my school."
The words float me into sleep.

"If you don't go to school on Monday you'll have to come on the dig with me," Dad says. "We're working on the site of an old shipwreck."

The face of the Seal-boy surges over me like a wave.

"I'm not digging for anything! But I'll go to school if you take me to the library today?"

"It's a deal!"

We walk along the beach in silence and stand on Corey's rock. I wonder if we'll ever walk straight on without thinking of him.

"I heard there is an angel called Magnus in your school," Dad jokes. I just stare at him. "You were sleep-talking!" he explains.

"Don't know what you're talking about."

"So there is no Magnus in your class?" Dad teases.

I don't answer.

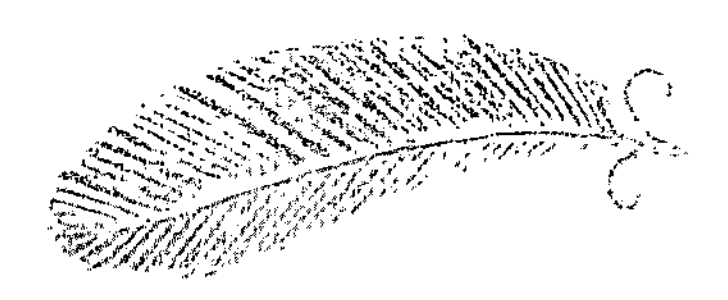

"I'll race you," he says. "Head start of ten."

I take off my shoes and socks and give them to Dad.

"Is this my handicap?"

I nod.

As soon as he's said the word we're thinking of the same thing.

How we always hated it when people called Corey that.

Mum's funeral words ring in my head.

'He slowed our lives down, and made us live every second.'

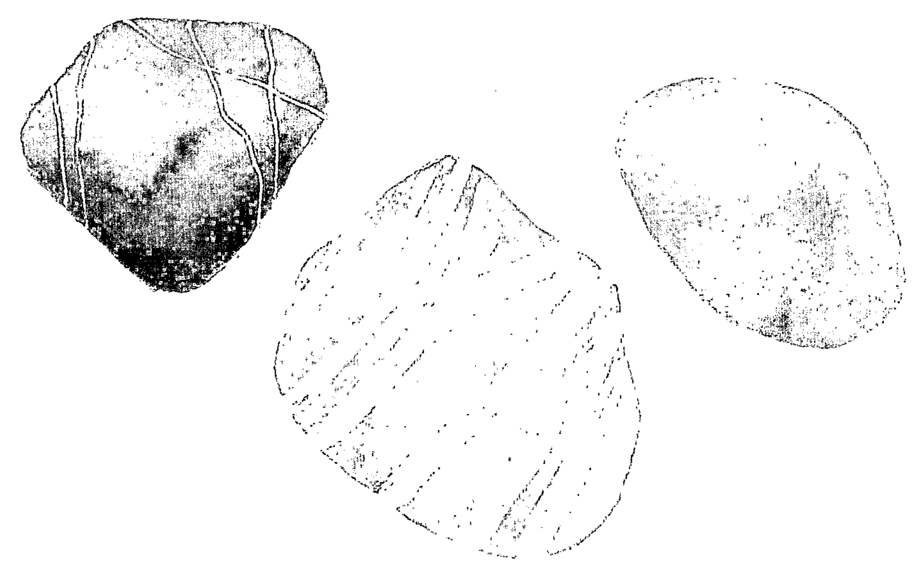

One, two, three.
I start to run, feel the wind in my hair and the sand between my toes.

At the library, two women stand at the counter, reading the newspaper.

"Breaks your heart, doesn't it, to see people washed in like pieces of driftwood, spewed up by the sea."

"Aye! I mean I was thinking the other day, what would make our family leave home to get on a leaky ship? You would have to be desperate."

I wait till they finish.

"How can I be of help? I don't think we've met."

"I'm Isla."

"Inga's wee one."

"Well, Corey was the youngest... but he's..."

The librarian looks like she might cry.

"We know, my love, we know!
Call me Lorna."

She nods towards her friend and smiles at me.
She knows, everyone knows. Magnus too.
Maybe they've all been told to be kind to me
because of Corey.
"Now then. What are you looking for today?"
"Selkie tales."

"Oh, I love it when the children want to know beyond their screens and games. It's all thumbs and fingers to me!" Lorna starts wiggling her thumbs and pretends to stare blankly at a screen.

"Would you believe I had my toddler group in the other day and one of the little 'uns tried to swipe a page over?" I laugh and follow her as she walks over to a shelf and collects a little stack of Selkie stories. "I like the ones with the paintings in."

"These should keep you going for a while!" Lorna points to some scatter cushions in a corner.

"You can have the sea-view to yourself if you want!" She points to the wall painting.

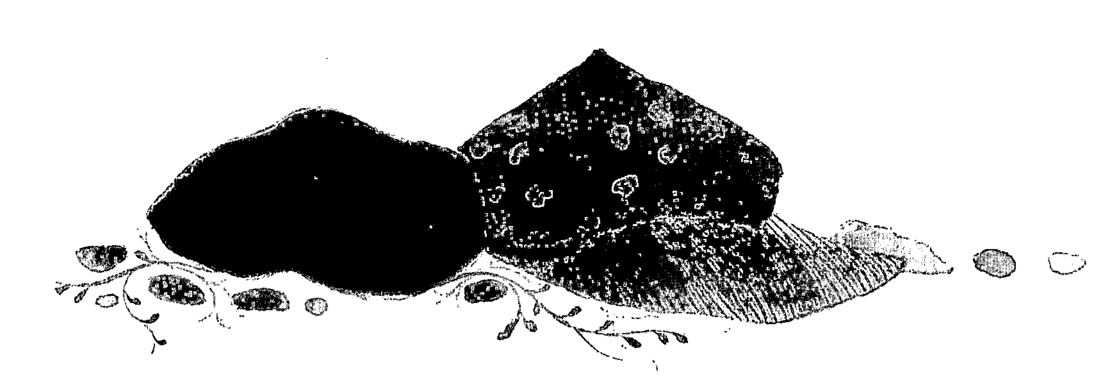

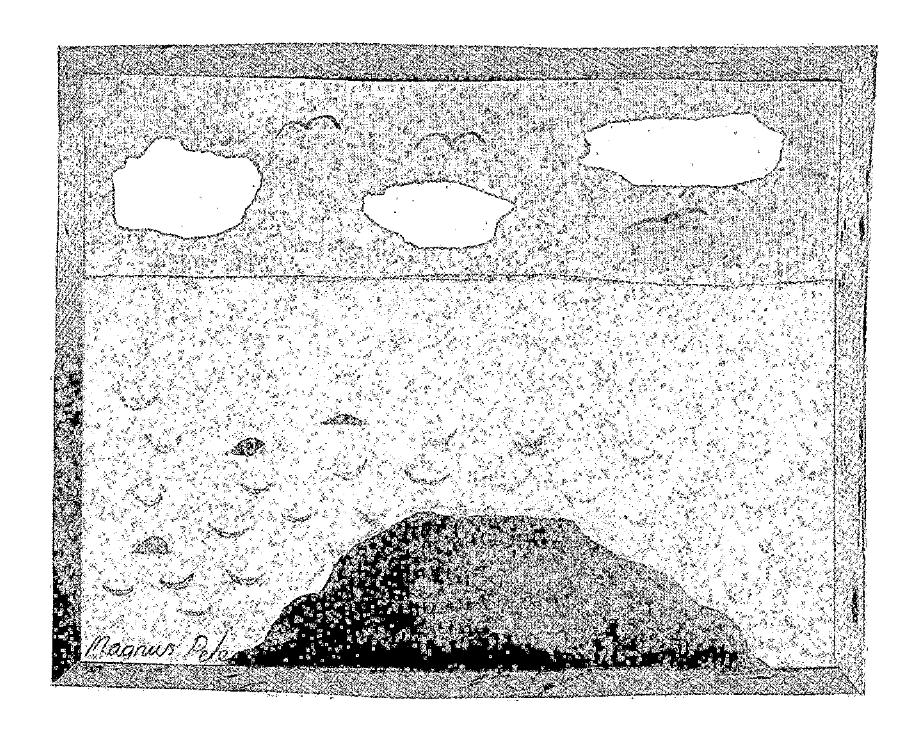

In the centre is Corey's rock.

"One of our young artists painted this for us. Pretty, isn't it?"

At the edge there is a name. *Magnus Peterson.*

Magnus P with his chipped tooth. Magnus who 'took salt to his lip'. Magnus who sits next to me in class has drawn this picture of Corey's rock.

I feel strange.

I lie down among the scatter-cushions and start to read, but the librarians' hushed whispers break in.

"Poor Inga, such a terrible loss and her a midwife too... Pretty little thing, isn't she? Beautiful skin. She's a look of Inga too."

I close my ears to them.

I am back on Corey's rock.

Listening to the waves crashing against the shore .

I turn the first page.

There are drawings of seals with human legs, seals with human faces.

'Some storytellers say the selkie-folk are actually the souls of those who drowned, and sometimes these lost souls are permitted to leave the sea for just one night and return to their original human form.'

The doctor said, when they couldn't help him any more, that his lungs were so full of water it was like drowning.

I need to get out of here.

I need to be on Corey's rock.

I take the book, leaving the others on the floor,

and head for the door.

On the way out I set a buzzer off and remember where I am.

"If you want to take this out you'll need a card. What's your full name?"

"Isla Angel Abiona."

I don't usually tell people the Angel bit.

"Beautiful sounding name, that – A-b-i-o-n-a."

Lorna spells it out and I nod to show she's got it right.

"Do you know what it means?"

"*Born on a journey*. I've got to go now!" I say.

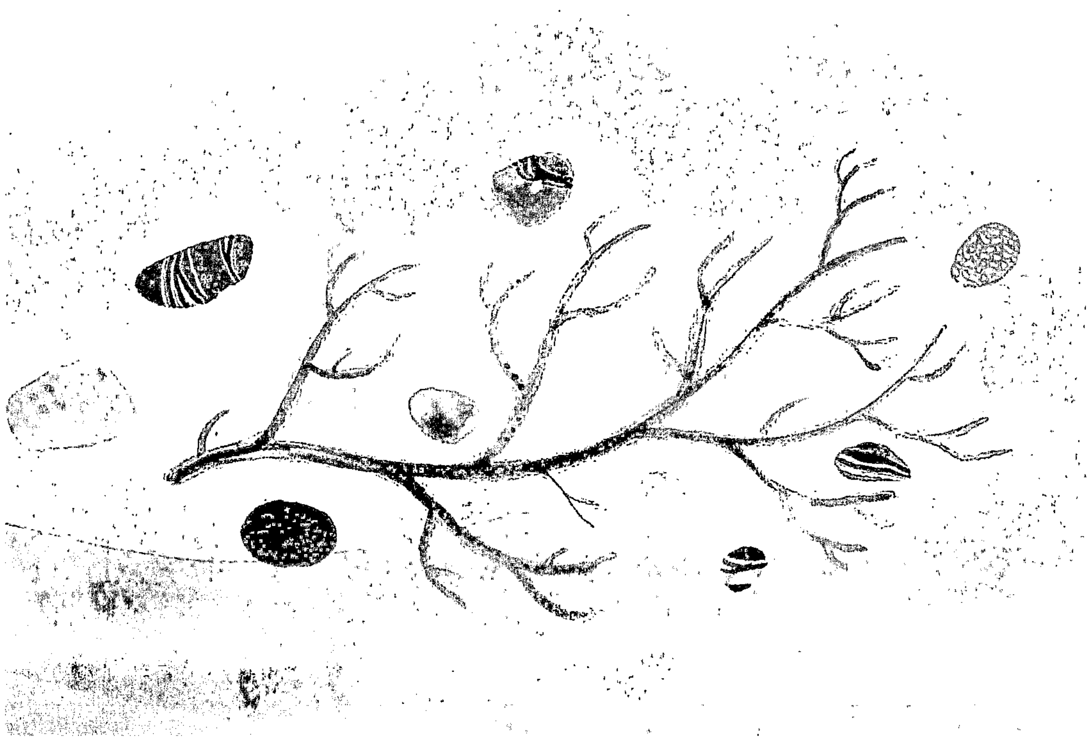

"Well, Isla Angel Abiona, you're very welcome here any time, and send my best to your parents from Library Lorna, that's what folk call me around here. Tell your mam and dad to come and see us."

I wait on the steps for Dad.

At least he doesn't insist on coming in and looking around.

"No secret rendezvous with Magnus then?" Dad says.

I bash him on the arm and he pretends it hurts. I don't tell him about Corey's rock or the sketch I keep in my pocket.

To Isla A, from Magnus P.

No starfish have washed in today.
Next to Corey's rock I stop and show Dad the Selkie book.
"You know Corey can't come back, don't you?" Dad sighs.
I won't answer him. I make a seal shape in the sand
and start to build its body up. Dad sits on Corey's rock
and watches the sea. It takes me a long time to get
the eyes right.

When it's done, Dad comes to look. "They do have human-looking eyes, don't they?"

My eyes are sore from reading.
The wind howls round the cottage roof.
Tomorrow there will be hundreds of starfish to save.

There's shouting and screaming. I look in the boat and everyone I know, Li-Mei and all my old schoolfriends, my teachers, my cousins, people in my new class, Miss Lachlan, Library Lorna, Mum, Dad, me and Corey are all being pushed out to sea on a boat.
The water starts to trickle in. Magnus is sitting next to me.
I watch his face become a seal's.
"'We'll have to jump!' Magnus-seal says, taking hold of my hand.
"But Corey can't swim," I call out.
I look over to him, being held close in Mum's arms.
The skin around his head begins to change colour. His thin legs that dangle over Mum's suddenly stir into life.
A seal tail flicks and he leaps off Mum's knee and into the cold, cold water.

The boat turns over and we are swimming down towards the sea bed, following a path of red petals.

Shhhhhh shhhhhh shhhhhhh

Someone is stroking my head over and over.

Like Mum used to.

I can smell her close.

I reach out for her hand without opening my eyes.

"It's OK, Mum. Corey can swim!" I tell her.

Shhhhh Shhhhhh Shhhhhhh

She kisses me on my forehead again.

I open my eyes as she leaves.

She's got dressed.

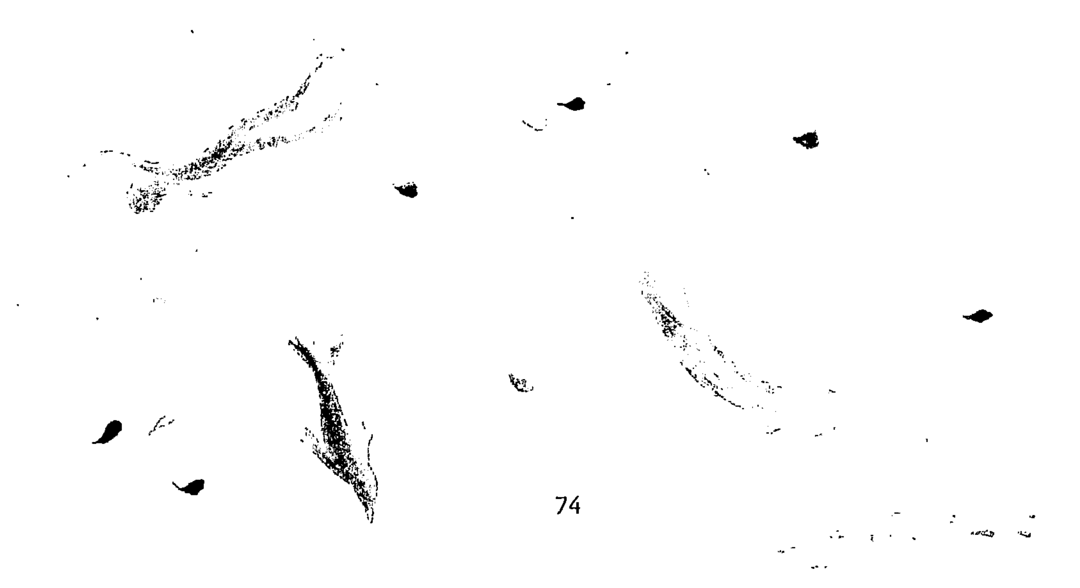

"Dreaming of Corey," I hear Mum tell Dad.

Their night-voices sound submerged in water.

Mum's worry-voice washes in.

"But I haven't delivered a baby for so long."

"Inga, my love. You've done it a thousand times before.

Why shouldn't it go well?"

Mum drives away, the headlights fade.

After, one, two, three, four, five....

Soon Dad's gentle snoring sounds through the walls.

I'm thirsty
I feel like I've swallowed the sea.
I climb out of bed, tiptoe down the stairs and sit at the table with a glass of milk.
I stare up at the photo of Mum holding me and Corey on her knee. The photo of us before the news about all the operations.
I shiver with cold and Sultan pads over to me.
There is still a glow in the wood-burner. I walk over, throw on a log and it springs into flame.
I take the grey shawl that was always Corey's and wrap it round my shoulders.
I sit in the chair where we rocked together.
Watch the flames dance in the fire.
Feel the heat warm my face.

A voice is calling to me in Yoruba.

I can only pick out a few words.

ègbon obìnrin

Sister, Mama, Sister, Mama.

Sultan pads over to the door and whines.

I open it.

"Corey, is that you?"

I move aside and the boy heads towards the fire, shivering.

He is naked. His hair and skin glisten with water.

I take the blanket from my shoulders and wrap it round his body.

"Mama," he says over and over as he sniffs at the blanket.

"Corey?" I ask, but he doesn't seem to know that name.

Sultan nuzzles up to him.

"Do you need food?" I ask.

I go to the cupboard and gets biscuits, but he shakes his head.

I offer him a glass of water but he shakes his head.

So I go over to him and pick him up just like I used to hold Corey,

and we rock all night in the chair as he twiddles my hair until we both fall asleep.

I climb upstairs and take the Selkie skin from the trunk.
He nods as if this is what he has been waiting for.
We walk to the door.
The boy keeps one hand on Sultan's back.
We are together, the three of us, on Corey's rock.
It's the moment just before sunrise when the birds feel the light stirring,
The wind has stilled.
The boy drops the blanket from his back and now I see the scars from all the operations are written on his body. He must be Corey.
Sultan sets up a whine that pierces my heart.
The boy kneels down and holds him.
Then he takes the Selkie skin and steps inside.

The scars are all gone now. The boy turns and all that is left is Corey's eyes. I reach for him and he leaps from the rock in a wide proud arch.

I watch the ripples on the flat water. Sultan watches too.

"What on earth are you doing here? You frightened the life out of me! I've been looking everywhere for you. Mum must have left the door open. You can't sleep here, you'll be ill."

Dad takes me in his arms and holds me close, watching the water. "No more sleep-walking."

I point to where a single grey seal raises its head in the distance, watches us for a while and then disappears.

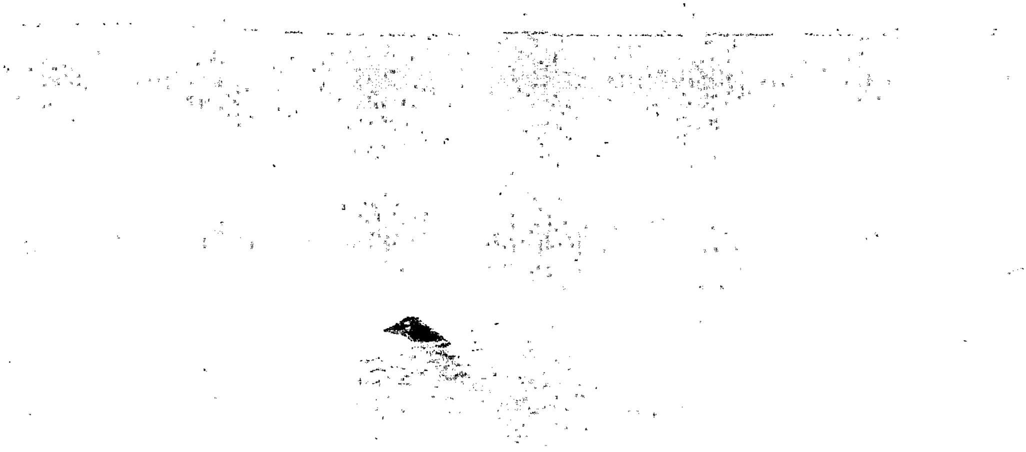

Dad stokes the burner, makes me a hot chocolate and toast and we sit together, wrapped in Corey's blanket, waiting for Mum.

The door opens and a bright spirit of happiness
blows in.
Mum is back.
I forgot that she used to scatter words everywhere.
"That's my first island baby brought into the world, safe and sound. You'll never guess who it was? Katherine Peterson. Used to sit next to her at school. Shame we lost touch really, we were remembering so many happy days."
"And the baby's fine?" Dad asks.
"Gorgeous little thing, he is."
When Mum says 'he is', her voice breaks on the words.

Dad walks over to Mum and wraps his arms around her shoulders.

"And you? Are you all right?"

Mum collapses onto the sofa.

"I slipped back into it and it all came to me. Lovely to see them so happy. They asked me to name him... and it just came out of my mouth that he should be called Corey. I hope you won't mind, will you? We had a good cry together."

Dad hugs Mum close.

"Oh, and Katherine has another boy. He said, 'Tell Isla Magnus says hello!'"

Dad winks at me and tickles me under my arm.

I squirm away and complain, but I have this feeling wrapped around us all, that I haven't felt for so long. Happiness.

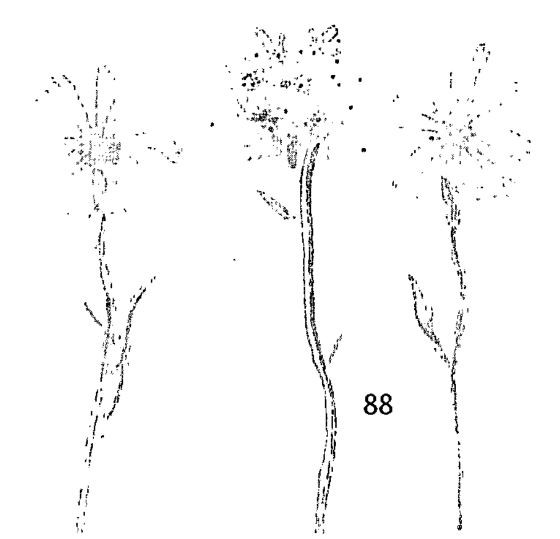

Mum says after she's been to visit baby Corey
she'll come to our Corey's rock with me today,
see if my sand-seal's still there or washed away.

The sky is so blue.
No clouds.
The sea is all of a silver glisten.
The cold bites into you with its brightness.
I run to Corey's rock with Sultan trailing behind,
puffing and panting.
As soon as I see the beach, I slow.
A boy is sitting on Corey's rock, silhouetted against
the sun.
I hold my breath as I walk towards him.

He turns his head.

"Hi, Isla A!"

"Hi, Magnus P."

"I met your mam last night. Did she say?"

I nod.

"I've got a brother, your mam named him Corey," Magnus tells me.

"I know," I say.

"Is that your Selkie?" he asks, looking at the seal sculpture I made in the sand.

I nod.

The tail has washed away.

"You've picked the best place on the island to spot seals. Want to come to mine to see the baby after?"

I smile. "Yes."

Magnus leans forward, dips his finger in the sea
and tastes.
"What are you doing that for?" I ask.
"Sometimes when I do, the seals come," he laughs.
We sit quiet while the sea whispers.
And in the distance one, by one, by one, by one...
by one...
seals rise from the waves.